To
Charles Valentine

The Okinawa Dragon

Nicola Monaghan

CRIME EXPRE/S

Five Leaves Publications,
PO Box 8786, Nottingham NG1 9AW
info@fiveleaves.co.uk
www.fiveleaves.co.uk

ISBN 978 1 905512 39 3

Crime Express 4

Five Leaves acknowledges financial support
from Arts Council England

Five Leaves is a member of Inpress
(www.inpressbooks.co.uk),
representing independent publishers

Typesetting and design:
Four Sheets Design and Print
Printed in Great Britain

Chicago O'Hare, Gate K9, 4.30am, Tuesday, November 25th, 2004. As space–time co-ordinates go, these pretty well suck ass.

I'm staring at the arrivals screen, hypnotised by the rhythms of its flicker, waiting for Henri. He's due off the red eye from Vegas and never has the term been so real to me. I feel like there's grit dripping from my lashes when I blink. The ETA on his flight is a random variable. It twitches and changes like the last traded price on a stock or share. I'd know all about that because I used to be a market maker for a big investment bank. They took me on 'cos I was sharp with maths and it took me no time at all to do the add-ups.

1. I was never gonna get rich working for someone else
2. You can make a market in anything

That's how come I ended up here; travelling halfway round the world to sell some collector a few pieces of cardboard.

It makes me laugh out loud.

I've been stood so long staring hard at the screen that I'm floating. I got that low blood sugar, frothy-headed feeling. I can see my legs giving way, imagine myself clattering to the ground like a wooden puppet. It's not just the watching and waiting; it's the airport thing.

I kinda like airports, which is just as well, but they fuck with my head. They're not one country or the next, like that place with the ponds in *The Magician's Nephew*. There's that eerie peace, a void echo. And other stuff. The sexy goodwill and edgy chimes of the recorded announcements. The promise of the destinations radiating from the screens and through my grey matter, leaving cells permanently changed: Prague, Tokyo, Dubai. Marrakesh via Casablanca.

Even going to the toilet screws with you; the automatic flush when you stand up and the taps, always willing to give water provided you offer up your hands in prayer to the god of laser beam technology.

The whole thing makes me feel like I walked through security and into the head of Philip K Dick.

And don't even get me started on the passengers. The calm acceptance in their eyes. The way they pile on to those huge metal monsters and allow themselves to get catapulted several thousand feet into the cold, wet air. It's enough to set my asthma off, watching them file through the gates.

I'm stood waiting, staring, and I need a wazz pretty darn bad but daren't move. What I think might happen if I do is undefined. Henri's flying domestic, so he won't have to go through all the questions about business or pleasure and cattle in his suitcase like I did, but it's still gonna take him a while to get through the gate and the baggage hall. This is the deal of my career, though; a fifty grand sale and the rarest collectible cards I've ever got my greasy little hands on.

How I got these very special items was a mutual back-scratching situation with this woman who works for the manufacturer. You don't need to know the details, all you need to know is she gave me the cards. Real collectors' pieces, real rare. She was very clear about the deal. *Here are the cards. You do not have the cards.*

Of course, we put something up on our website toot sweet. Not pictures or anything that cheeky. Just a little note; descriptions of the cards. *We heard these exist, "waaaay" cool. Man, they must be worth ten grand a piece.*

I knew someone would bite and I would have put money on it being Henri. He's the most powerful collector I know. Must have just about all there is to get by now, first edition playsets, sealed product from forever back. I'd love to see his stash but I don't know him well enough to ask.

Maybe after this deal.

My need to pee is making me dance so I give in and head to the loos. Of course, when I get back, the sparrow has landed. Innit always the way? It's like the cigarette rule; derived by first principles from Sod's law. Whatever you're waiting for, a bus, train, your main course at a posh restaurant, just light up a fag and, no matter how late it is, or how unlikely it seemed that you'd ever see it, along it will come. I've tried and tested this all over the world and it just works lol.

So, I'm dashing back to the gate to head him off, so eager am I. Then I'm waiting there for at least five minutes, though it feels more like an hour. I'm sighing and strutting and looking at my watch.

Henri arrives. When I see him, the usual stuff hits me. How small he is, around five–six and adolescent skinny. The way he dresses in jeans and a T-shirt, threadbare sports jacket. The flecks of grey in his mid-brown hair and his

9

careful way of moving. He doesn't look like a millionaire.

He nods in my direction, then leads the way to one of those anonymous coffee bars you get in airports. I have a latte, but Henri takes one of those small dark coffees so full of grounds they're thick as oil. He adds three sugars and stirs the evil concoction with some vigour. It is these small details that make him so very European. Me, I'm from the 51st state, innit?

So, we sit on high wooden chairs and Henri asks if he can see the photo. This is how on-it the man is; he didn't even dream I'd bring the cards. I dip my head and scan the room, then pull it from my inside pocket. The whole thing is so B-movie it makes me cringe.

The picture is of Uri, my business partner. He's holding the cards (in protective sleeves of course) fanning them out in one hand and pointing at them with the other, one of those grins plastered over his ugly mug where you can see chinks of light hit his teeth.

'You bring one?' Henri asks.

The guy's so sharp it's a surprise he's not a

mess of scars. I go into my pocket again and bring out the sample. Henri takes the card from me and removes it from its plastic sleeve like he's carrying out a surgical procedure. He examines it, front and back, takes a magnifying glass from his pocket and has a look real close.

I'm sweating.

He puts the card back inside its protective cover and passes it back. He nods, half smiles.

I hand him the small piece of paper I prepared earlier. Sort code, bank account number, a figure in sterling.

I'm sweating like a rapist.

He looks lost in his head for a moment or so, then he nods again, firmly this time.

'Bah, it's a good price,' he says.

I smile at Henri, playing it cool, but inside my head I'm running round in circles, doing a little victory dance. But that's for my eyes only.

Deal cut, I sit against the chair back and the way it feels is like I must visibly relax, my head swinging back, tummy pushing out. It strikes me for a second that this might make me look amateur. But I don't care. I am flying.

We get chatting then. About the cards, the game. Henri tells me about some of the things he has and I make all the right noises. I talk tournament play and collectibles and I can hear myself going psycho with the words per minute. Henri doesn't seem to mind. We have more coffee and my heart is racing along with the words. He smiles and nods and I can tell he admires my energy. People do.

We talk about his collection and he gives me a run down. It has two parts; public and private. The latter, he tells me, is kept to himself and a few close associates, to protect the not so innocent. He mentions a couple of cards and that's when I understand Henri is more than a millionaire. He is someone who is capable of making me a millionaire. And so I have to ask him because you can't miss opportunities like this.

'Is there anything you're looking for now, that you haven't got? I mean anything at all you need to complete your collection?'

Henri looks at me. Laughs. 'There's not much left,' he says. 'Not much but the odd thing like this if you find it. And, of course, *The Dragon.*'

I perk up like some kinda meerkat. He doesn't need to say which dragon. Okinawa is a legend in our business, the Mona Lisa of the cards. Given as a gift to some Japanese businessman. You can't buy it off him; he doesn't need the money and the Japanese honour code says you don't sell a gift. *It is written.*

'How much?' I say. 'How much would you pay for a piece like that?'

Henri bats the air, grins. His eye contact goes but I am still looking right at him. 'Is unobtainable, impossible,' he says, with a fluff of a laugh.

I do not laugh. I wait for his eyes to come back to me and stare straight into them.

'Nothing is impossible.'

Amsterdam Schiphol, a bright, clear afternoon in December. Henri must have a thing about airports because we could have met anywhere. We could have met in a coffee shop in town, had a smoke. I am mourning this opportunity lost as I see him appear through the gate, minus the pull along bag he had with him last time.

He's flown here just to get the cards.

When I tell people I deal in these gaming cards they stare back with a blank look on their face, or come out with some bland statement like 'Is there money in that?' Last week Henri paid just short of fifty grand into my offshore account and I am here to give him his cardboard.

Things are worth what people are prepared to pay for them.

We go to a bar this time and I'm buying. Henri takes a pastis with just a drop of water, so strong that I smell the aniseed each time he lifts it up to his mouth. I have a tall, cold beer. First, I give him a couple of sweeteners. Little gifts from me and Uri to add a bit of value. He examines the gem mint, rare cards and smiles. 'Nice,' he says. Then I cut to the chase and get the test cards from my bag.

Henri takes them from me like they're his new born kids. He extracts them from sleeves and examines them one by one. He smiles and places them in a small plastic box, then tucks that away in his briefcase. He gives me a broad smile and shakes my hand.

'Good doing business with ya,' I say.

'Likewise, young man.'

I take a huge swallow of my drink and almost choke on it, then propose a toast. I wave at the barman for another round.

Henri's flight back to Paris CDG is not for a few hours so we drink and talk and I can hear my words per minute go right off the scale. Henri is quiet. He sits back and listens mostly, cuts in with the odd wise comment. I wonder if this ability to observe is what has made him so rich. I know I miss stuff 'cos I'm restless and end up all over the place. Energy has its downside.

I never miss an opportunity, though. It's when Henri's voice is slurring slightly and he lights a cigar that I mention it. *The Dragon.*

He laughs and shakes his head. Calls me a madman.

'In theory, though,' I say. 'How much in theory?'

He flicks ash and blows out silver rings, as if

even his breath carries precious metal.

'In theory,' I say, 'if someone was willing to go to Japan and scope out the deal. Find *The Dragon* and work out how to, let's say, acquire it. I mean, would you pay someone to do that?'

Henri nods. He writes a figure in the air with the end of his cigar, each digit burning into the space between us. I take the wet doily from underneath my drink and clarify in pen. The ink bleeds.

I breathe in deep

Henri nods at what I've written down and I make blue circles grow from the pen nib until it's all blotted out. 'In theory,' he says, 'would the payment details be the same?'

'In theory,' I say. And I wink.

Osaka International, and fuck knows what time it is here, there, everywhere. I am seriously disoriented, the way you get when you pass through enough time zones. I can never sleep on flights and my eyes are so red I look like the devil from a low budget movie. If someone fucked me off I could just throw them a wide stare and they'd wet their pants.

It's less than two weeks since my meeting with Henri in Schiphol; I'm an iron hot kinda guy.

I've been stood at the baggage carousel for what feels like an age. Cases pass me by, that jolly fucking merry-go-round. I stand there wondering how much I give a shit about my stuff turning up. Thanks to my mate Henri, I could kit myself out a hundred times over, the cheap jean and t-shirt taste I got.

Problem is, my blueprints are in that bag. Maps, plans, names — all the information I figured I'd need to get going with this job. Careless, now I think about it. I should have pinned them underneath my clothes and travelled with them next to my skin. Note to self: Never leave your masterplan unattended. As I see each group from my flight leave with bags and mine's still not there, I get the fear. Then there's just me left and the belt's moving round and round and all I see is black rubber. Finally, there's a sound of creaky levers and pulleys and the fucking thing stops, and the display changes from *London Heathrow* to *Frankfurt am Main*.

I swallow my heart as it jumps right up into my throat.

All I want to do right now is check into my hotel and collapse into my bed. But I know, if I leave, that bag's gone for good. My arms fall limply to my sides. I feel like crying.

Then I look up and see this brunette coming at me. Sheer bloody tiredness makes it feel like this is all in my head, a desert mirage or pure imagination. I watch her hair bounce up and down as she walks; it looks like an out-take from a shampoo ad. She's tall, with slim legs, wearing something that doesn't quite meet my definition of a dress and a very naughty smile. *Rowr!* The way she looks diverts my attention from what she's carrying for a moment. What she's carrying is my bag.

I do a cartoon double take.

'I think I took the wrong one. By mistake,' she says. She has an English accent, cut glass, reminding me of bad women in worse movies. And she is kinda familiar too. Maybe she is an actress, one of the C list types who play these parts. I can't quite place her, though.

I stare with an open mouth as she speaks, trying to take it all in. 'Thanks,' I say, and she hands me the bag. Then she's off, turning back a few yards away to give me one last, dirty-looking smile. I watch her hips sway as she leaves the arrivals hall. It's only when her pert ass has left the room that it strikes me. How did she know it was my bag? Okay, so she could have guessed that, given I was the only person here still waiting. But if she'd been on my flight, why hadn't I noticed her before? She was the sort of woman I would notice. And she walked right out of here without any bag, no sign of the other one she'd supposedly mistaken mine for, and no sign of her making any effort to find it. I shake myself out of the trance she's put me in and open the case, check everything's there. My clothes look neatly folded; they can't have been moved and put back that way in the time she had. My papers are in the pouch where I hid them, thank Christ, and my spare inhaler's still tucked under the elastic at one side.

Everything looks in order but I can feel it in

my gut; she was too damn good looking, and too undressed. Like something sent by mail order just to make my dick hard. I may be thousands of miles from the state of Denmark, but something is rotten, for sure.

My head was dropping in the taxi the entire journey from the airport to my hotel. I'd booked a room in the Swissotel, because it's A. in the thick of things and B. a great hotel. One of the best things about this business is getting to stay in really good hotels. I've done the Ritz Carlton and the Four Seasons in New York, the Arts in Madrid. I've done the Paris Hilton too, but that joke's too easy so I'm not going to go there lol. There's nothing to match cool Egyptian cotton against your skin on a warm night (except perhaps Paris). Besides, you're ten times more likely to get the girl you're hitting on to come back to your room if it's inside a building with five stars stuck on front; if you have a mini bar fully loaded with champagne and you're prepared to use it.

I walk into the lobby, which is chilled like the inside of a fridge and has a high ceiling. There's a young Japanese girl sitting at the reception desk. She's staring me out. Checking me out, maybe, pardon the pun. Western guys are hot here. And don't start me on Japanese women. They just do something for me. The girlie clothes they wear, the frothy accoutrements like beads and bangles. Their willowy slim figures and easy laughs, the eager accommodating way they look at you. *Rowr!*

I'm too tired to flirt though, and just hand her the print out of my booking. She smiles, asks for ID and gives me a key card and instructions of how to find my room. I'm only half listening.

I get in the lift to the 3rd floor and search for 324. I walk. And I walk and I walk. I'm dying to crash out and stay dormant till morning but I'm still walking. Then I find my room. It's about as far from the lift as it could feasibly be. This always happens to me.

I push the card into its hole in the door and it doesn't unlock first time. I'm almost ready to kick it open. I place the card in again and hear the click of the catch being released. I walk in, dumping my troublesome bag, then throw myself on the bed, expecting oblivion.

But it doesn't come.

Something about my body clock has kicked in. That and the adrenaline from nearly losing my suitcase, and it being returned by *The Girl*. I smile as I think about the dress she was almost wearing. If I wasn't so exhausted, I'd have a wank over that. My eyes ache for proper rest but it's like they're glued open. It's all like something straight out of that movie, *Lost in Translation*.

I lie there for half an hour and then I know it's not going to happen. Another downside of that energy of mine. I know from experience it's a stupid waste of time chasing sleep like this. I might as well make the most of it. I get out of bed and open the curtains. It's dark out there.

This helps me tell the time. Party time!

Some random bar, Osaka, 9.30pm, steaming drunk. I've been drinking flaming Sambucas with whisky chasers. My fatigue has made the drinks go to my head that much faster, but I'm getting a feel for space time again.

It's then I have a typical Jack Casey bright idea. Karaoke!

I like to do things like this. Eat pizza in Italy and Tapas in Spain, hot dogs from a street vendor in Times Square. I have a mate who has this inverted snobbery about shit like this. He won't go to a bar where they serve beer in the right glasses. But I laugh in the face of such hardships.

I stagger out of the bar and into the street, and I have to ask a few people before I find someone who understands enough English to help me. Actually, I think the only word he's actually mastered is 'Karaoke'. He keeps repeating this back to me, and pointing straight into the sky and yet vaguely in the direction of a nearby building, saying 'Ay, ay! Karaoke! Happy!'

'Thank you,' I tell him, smiling. 'Karaoke Happy!' And I give him a big thumbs up.

The bloke inside the tower block doesn't understand a word of English. I mime singing into a microphone and he gets all excited, pointing to the lift and shouting something. More miming from both of us, as well as pointing at the list on the wall, and we establish I need to go to the fourteenth floor and turn left, then left again (I think). Not a place that relies on passing trade, then.

I follow his directions and come to a sign written in Japanese on the front of what looks like an office. From outside, the place seems quiet, with no audible sign of either the Karaoke, or the Happy. Then I push open the door and the sound hits me.

I grin my little head off.

I pay my in and walk through to the bar. I'm greeted by a small Japanese girl. She cocks her head and gives me a smile. I grin back. 'Hello babe,' I say, and she giggles, placing a tiny curled hand over her mouth. I can tell by the way she laughs that she didn't understand me. She gestures to a table that is already half full of beery looking western men. And I think, yeah, that'll be more fun than sitting on my own.

I sit down and meet Ted, Chuck and Marc, American ex-pats working for a bank here.

They are fabulously leery and beery for yanks, and we hit it off from the go. They each have a petite Japanese girl of their own. Our Japanese girls bring us drinks, pour out our beer for us and clap and cheer like mad things when we sing. They laugh ridiculously when we make jokes, and some of them say 'very funny' in that can't quite pronounce the consonants way, and you can tell they have no idea what the words mean. The yanks get a bit cruel about this, saying stuff like 'stupid bitch' to each other, and laughing, then pissing themselves when the girls come out with 'very funny' and their weird fake giggles. Me, I'm torn between being fabulously turned on by the experience, and worried that there's something not quite right here. The more beer I have, the less I worry.

A group of Japanese men walk in, and girls appear from nowhere to greet them. They take them to the table across from us. They are all wearing suits and I suspect they've come straight from work. They sit and order drinks, talking quietly. They look as though they've been here many times before. One of them gets up to sing. We're all loving his interpretation of 'I like the way you move' and his dancing, well, it was 'very funny'.

The yanks take turns to sing Bon Jovi songs, but they're being ironic. They shout into the mics and air guitar and do the arched back, penis thrusting singing poses favoured by such soft rock giants. I choose Red Hot Chili Peppers, and enjoy the stomping. The yank boys are silenced by the fact I can actually sing. They weren't counting on that. My little girl goes crazy with the clapping and cheering when I finish, and I almost think she might mean it. The boys thump me on the back and give me meaty grins.

It's when I get up to piss that things get really strange. My girl follows me. I try to explain to her where I'm going, miming and everything, but she just nods and giggles and continues to follow me. She goes right into the wash room with me and I'm starting to worry she's planning to hold my dick while I piss. The place is tiny and we have to stand close to fit in together; we're almost touching. I'm not sure whether to feel excited or embarrassed. She doesn't follow me into the cubicle, and now I'm not sure whether to feel relieved or disappointed.

I piss, thinking how loud it sounds, and how long I go on for, and how I can hear her breathing outside. I hold back a fart. I go out to find she has switched on the tap, and is smiling at me. I put my hands into the water and she soaps them, rubbing and cleaning until the water runs clear. Then she grabs the soft white towel and pats my hands dry. It's a sensual experience, but it doesn't feel sexual. It's like a head massage at a really good hairdressers. Am I supposed to tip her now? I don't have cash with me. It didn't even cross my mind that she would follow me here.

I head back over to the table, my girl tottering after me. It's time to move off the beer and onto vodka. I take it straight, and it's brought over by my *Very Funny* girl in a small neat glass, frosted with salt and with a mint garnish. This place is conscientious about the way it serves drinks. It's also brutally expensive if the little look I took at the cocktail menu is anything to go on. My tab must be getting pretty darn serious at this point. Thank fuck for Henri.

I order another.

I ask everyone else if I can get them a drink.

Yes, thank fuck for Henri, and for the *Okinawa Dragon*. I'm drunk enough that remembering the purpose of my trip sends a thrill right through me. I make my mind up to get completely wasted tonight. I am short of time. Japan's a real Cinderella country — eleven o'clock strikes and everything closes and you're out on the streets.

Then Marc's beckoning me to move in and listen. 'You wanna come back to our apartment and drink some more?'

I take about three seconds to decide.

11.13pm, streets of Osaka, following three drunken Americans who appear to be performing some kinda random walk. As predicted, we were ushered out of the doors at eleven on the dot. Marc said his place was a five minute walk, but we're still walking and there's no sign yet of any place residential.

We arrive at a high rise, and the boys head in. It's a pretty impressive building. Typical flash kinda place that tends to be the abode of choice for these banker types. The lobby is all marble and high ceilings. Our footsteps sound loud and unfettered as they shatter the silence. Ted makes some joke about an English bloke asking for fags at an American service station and there's an explosion of laughter. It sounds harsh, inappropriate. As we head to the lift I get a sense of déjà vu. I'm reminded of the Matrix and life isn't feeling real anymore. I feel out of body. Maybe it's the alcohol, or the jetlag, or just the fact I haven't slept in about twenty-four hours, but I can't totally tell whether I'm awake, or asleep and dreaming. I know there's a test you can do to tell, something about actions and consequences which get fucked up in a dream, but I'm too out of it to remember how it works. So I just follow Jack to the lift.

Next I know, we're on the 32nd floor. Definitely a room with a view. You can see the harbour at Kobe from here, its curves lit by decorated buildings. There's a radio tower, and a structure the shape of Sidney Opera House. It looks too good; like a fake view has been painted on the window.

Someone somewhere has lit a joint because I can smell it. I'm sniffing it out, trying to get in on smoking the thing. I find the source of the beautiful aroma; Ted sitting on a bed in the spare room. I park myself next to him and he does the polite thing, passing on the joint. I take three deep drags, then pass it back. I lie back on the bed and my head is spinning. Someone has put on music, something 90s with heavy, grinding guitar, Nirvana I think. The chatter and laughter from the living room seems way too much for three people. It sounds like a party. I'm tempted to get up off the bed and go back in there, but here is where the weed is. Besides, I'm not sure I could move if I wanted to. I think I might be sick if I tried. All I can see is the hallway, inverted. So I lie there, taking the odd drag more when I get passed the doobie and listening in to the silly talk in the other room. You know the kinda shit. The rudeness of Captain Pugwash, and the story of the woman who was bitten by a spider and had lots of baby ones erupt from the sore. The usual urban myths that come out when strangers get together overseas. I feel like I've slipped over dreamside and that nothing is real.

And that's when I see her — the incredibly hot suitcase-stealing bitch from the airport. She's in the hallway, and I watch her through the door. She puts on her coat. I know she's leaving and I want to go after her but I cannot move. Some kinda drug/alcohol/emotionally induced paralysis has set in. Perhaps I have lapsed into a coma. Whatever it is, I cannot get up and follow her.

All I can think is that I'm either dreaming or hallucinating and I don't mind because there are worst thing to conjure up out of nowhere. I think about those awake/dreaming tests again. I consider getting up and following *The Girl*, checking whether she is real or not.

But I am stuck to the bed.

I feel surprisingly fresh when I wake up the next day. Bright and breezy. No sign of the hangover I surely deserve. It's about seven in the morning and, although I'm not totally sure what time I fell asleep, I do remember hearing the expensive clock built into the wall strike four in the morning.

I wake up needing a piss and a drink, in that order. I head for the bathroom, trying to avoid standing on the two other blokes who've crashed on the floor. I have a memory of more people turning up here last night, but it's vague, and I don't recognise the men on the floor.

There's someone asleep in the bath, but I ignore him as I take a piss. My thirst is now raging, and I wash my hands then take a drink straight from the tap. The guy in the bath stirs a little, but he doesn't wake up. I head back into the living room. The curtains are open and I can see the bay. The sun is rising at the back of it, making bright orange streaks across a deep blue backdrop. It looks like art; it could have come straight off one of the cards. Looking at it reminds me of *The Dragon* and my reason for being here.

That thought fresh in my head, I find my trainers and jacket and head off. Outside the air is crisp and fresh. It's a pleasure to feel its sharp hit in my lungs. I walk at a brisk pace to stay warm. I'm feeling good. I'm stepping on all the cracks in the pavement and I couldn't give a shit. I think about the things I need to do. Case out the job. Make the relevant appointment with President Reito. These things will involve a visit to the headquarters of Isuchoto Games and a good deal of bullshit. I have my story prepared. I'm almost looking forward to it.

There's one last piece of the puzzle to sort out. I cannot turn up there in my usual attire, no matter how cool the T-shirt. One of the many advantages of what I do is that I can wear what I want. I hate formal clothes – they're just not me. But I will make an exception for this job. I will make all sorts of exceptions for this particular order. It's time to spend some more of Henri's cash.

Back at my hotel, I eat a big breakfast and drink enough coffee to get my leg twitching in my seat. Then I find the concierge, who can speak broken English. I ask him about the nearest shops, pointing at the garments I am wearing to indicate it's clothes I am looking for. He puts me in a taxi and tells it where to go. The cab stops in a glamorous looking street, and the driver sits there mute. I look at the number on his meter and hand him the right amount of yen. It astounds me always, how much can be achieved with no common words.

I wander up and down the street. Most of the shops are ridiculously trendy. The sort of clothes even models look stupid in. I wonder how the way I'm dressed led the concierge to think this was the right street for me. I walk a long way before I find a shop selling formal suits. I stand looking in the window for a while. Stiff, nasty clothing like this was an influence on my choice not stick with the *proper* job. Well, that and the working for other people and having a boss thing.

I take a deep breath, push open the door and walk right in as if I own the place. The assistant looks at me doubtfully. I smile and give the guy a thumbs up, then walk around the shop browsing the rails. I see what he's getting at. Holding the suit trousers against me, they reach to just below my knees. The jacket's going nowhere near me, not over my shoulders or anywhere near as far down my arms as my wrists. I am a totally different size and shape from your average Japanese bloke.

Just being near these suits is making my skin itch. The smell of the material makes me feel sick too. The assistant is scrambling around under his desk looking for something. I doubt somehow he's going to find a suit my size down there. He toddles over with a card in his hand, which he gives to me. He speaks to me in Japanese, getting louder when it's clear I don't understand a word. He grabs my arms and pulls me towards the door. He's a slight man, but much stronger than he looks. Outside he points and gestures and speaks in a very loud voice. He hands me the card and points again and is getting very excited. Then I see it. Another suit shop.

The other shop is across the road and I head straight for it. There are people backed up at the crossing, which is on red. Nothing is coming but no one is moving, one of the things that always makes me smile in Japan. Everyone here is just so damn obedient. *It is written*. It's cute and I'm probably very condescending, but that's how it makes me feel. Still, my destination in sight, I push through the crowd and cross the road, eliciting a couple of tuts and one gasp.

This shop is not so classy. The suit material is more poly than cotton and I can feel the static as I run my fingers down a sleeve. Still, the biggest items here will fit me. This must be the Japanese 'Big and Tall'. I pick a dark blue suit, and pale blue shirt, collarless. I draw the line at wearing a tie. This shop sells shoes too, ones my size, proof that it is a specialist outfitter because footwear is something I struggle with even back home. I buy some shiny black numbers and think how I will enjoy throwing the bastards down the rubbish chute once this whole thing is done.

And I am set. I have all the tools I need.

Suited and booted for the first time in years, the stiff material of my brand new shirt is making me itch. I got a skin condition. You'd probably never know it, except if you looked closely at the backs of my wrists, or the creases in my elbow and saw the little red spots and dry patches. If left untreated it gets angry, the skin itching, then swelling, welts and cuts forming when I can't help but scratch. Little round blood clots shine from under my skin, following the marks made by my nails, like chains of rubies. The doctors have all sorts of explanations. Eczema, dermatitis, psoriasis, over the years it's been all these things. I know the truth, though. It's a demon, living inside me, under my skin, trying to scratch its way out. Mu ha ha haaaa!

How it's treated is that I have to add this special oily mess to my bath called emollient. I have to spread on a thin layer of steroid lotion, then slap on a load of this thick, heavy cream. The net result of all this skin softening, all this moisturisation, is that my bathroom, my house, my life for fucksake, everything is covered in a fine sheen of oil. Slippery. It makes handling the cards tricky sometimes, because they'd be ruined by even one dab of this greasiness. When

I'm working, I have to wash my hands about three times an hour.

So I'm scratching at my neck as I approach the reception desk and the woman there is staring at me. I don't like the look of her; she isn't my target audience at all. I was hoping for a young woman, who might giggle with her hand over her mouth and give me what I want. I guess I was hoping for a *Very Funny* girl. Instead, the woman behind the counter is middle-aged, with thin pursed lips and sour eyes. As I approach, she appraises me from behind the glasses that sit towards the end of her nose. She looks disgusted to see me.

I give out my best, biggest, toothy grin and the receptionist's mouth smiles back, but her other muscles stay where they are, making her curled lips look like they've been stuck onto the front of her face.

'I have an appointment with President Reito,' I tell her.

She checks her book, looks up at me, confused. There is no record, there, I know. I rub my palms together and they slip against each other. I scratch my neck again.

'I spoke to his secretary Miss Nakamura. I have an amazing new game to show him. My bosses at Bro Toys UK will be really unimpressed if the admin here has messed up again,' I say.

She puts down her pen and fixes me with a firm look. 'Admin here is me, Sir, and I do not mess up.' Her English is impeccable; she doesn't even have an accent. I suspect she is as efficient as she claims. I also know I will get nowhere with her.

I continue to protest, but without any real conviction. She looks down at her papers and gets on with her work, as if I wasn't there. 'Fine,' I say. 'But you'll be hearing more about this.'

The woman looks up then, and smiles. She knows I am lying. I know she will never let me in.

I pick up my briefcase, toss my hair and storm out of the door.

I'm down but not out. A mere set back. I buy some sushi and a Coke, and sit on a bench near to the office block. I watch the comings and goings and whistle a happy tune. Plan B: Hope that the sour faced old prune works shifts and wait to see the switch over. Hopefully to some young, lithe woman who will be impressed by a Western man and do everything she can to help me. Or, failing that, who I can bully to my will. I know how to work these things. I know how to work pretty well everything except middle-aged women. Middle-aged women are too smart; they have seen so much and they don't want to have sex with me, and that is *no good*.

Two hours and several bento boxes later (I can be patient when I put my mind to it) I luck out. I hear the clip clip of high stilettos. The woman who owns these shoes has perfect posture and, as she comes past me, I recognise her as *Sour Face*. I did not see who came to replace her but I head in again, ready to take my chances.

My hopes dance in my chest as I walk towards the desk. Exactly what I'd ordered; young, impressionable, very cute. She throws me come to bed eyes all the way across the marble floor and I try to catch them. *Rowr!*

I crash my case down in front of her. 'I have an appointment with President Reito,' I tell her. Like her colleague before, she checks the book, then looks confused. But this time I'm pretty sure, if I'm indignant enough, that I will get what I want. Her confusion has an air of panic about it. She looks through her lashes at me and I feel twitches in my groin.

'It's just not good enough,' I say. I am almost stamping my foot. I have to admit, I am enjoying playing masterful with her.

'I can put you in the diary for tomorrow afternoon, for two o'clock,' she tells me.

I sigh, I tut. I roll my eyes. Then I say that I suppose it will have to do, and pick up my briefcase ready to storm from the building.

Result. Exactly what I'd hoped for.

I do a little dance, once I'm out of sight of the building, and this one's there for anyone to see.

You'd think lack of sleep would be cumulative. That it would pile up against you and eventually, like Rip Van Winkle, you're off to bed for a hundred years. But it doesn't work like that.

Especially when the next day you have the kinda plans I had. Those kinda plans keep your head buzzing and your heart banging and it's pretty darn hard to even think about sleep.

I came in from my adventures around 6pm, feeling fucked and with plans to crash. But I've been in bed for hours and I don't know where the fatigue has gone. My heart's ticking like a clock, like it's timing my race for sleep. And I'm lying there, aiming hard at unconsciousness, thinking that I really ought to keep trying given what I gotta do tomorrow. But I can hear my pulse in my ear. I can feel it vibrate my chest. I turn onto one side, lie all foetal, thinking 'this is comfy, this time I'll sleep' until twenty minutes later my arm is going dead and I flip to the other side and the same thing happens again. And again. AND AGAIN.

I sit up in bed. I'm gonna be red-eyed Jack again and there's nothing to be done about it. I might as well embrace it down in the hotel bar.

Shower, piss, a generous spray with deodorant, enough to make my head spin a little. It's a good feeling. The marble of the bathroom floor feels cold against my feet and it's all like a dream, like a dream, like a dream. I pull on a random t-shirt and my jeans from the day before, and head down into the night.

The hotel bar is littered with sad-looking businessmen, most of them Japanese. It's a depressing little place, but they sell beer. I find myself a table alone, and an English newspaper, and sit there with Asahi Super Dry. I kick back in the chair, and feel restful, and wonder if, after this drink, I might be able to sleep after all.

Two Asahis later and all thought of sleep has gone. I am busy wondering what mischief I can get up to in Osaka on a Thursday evening. I wouldn't mind some weed; that'd be fun and it would help me sleep, but I know from experience that scoring any kinda drugs in Japan is close to impossible. The place is just so damn clean. Good clean, though, you gotta admit. And so employed you gotta admire that. They pay people here to wave at your train, see you off on your morning commute. Everyone has a function and people are happier. You can see it.

There are no bums on the streets asking for your spare change. Maybe they just shoot 'em, who knows, but it's not something you see here.

I leave the hotel and head into the city lights. They're so pretty. I love being in big cities; I love their lightshows, and how you can see, on the roads approaching, a glow of life rising into the sky. I still remember being a baby, when all this was new to me, how alien the whole world felt. Japan still feels that way.

I pass a couple of sad looking bars, places that are wilting at the edges. Men in crumpled suits sit drinking beers and I don't fancy joining them. In the distance, I hear a repetitive, child-ish tune, up down scales and all over, like someone is dancing to make it. I know right away it's a computer game, something retro. And then I know exactly where I will while away my night.

Japanese arcades just piss on what you get in the rest of the world, as do the gamers here. I follow the sounds to their source. Inside, the noise is all over the place. The plink plink tunes of slots being won or lost, and of Mario and Pac

Man, just make themselves heard over the blast of machine guns, the roar of engines, screeching rock guitar and Britney Spears. I can hear the bubbling chink of metal balls. Pachinko!

I walk round and have a good look, then settle to watch the DDR experts on the dance mats. They fall into two categories; those who dance with style and occasionally miss the spots, and those who hit the right sensor on the mat every time, but don't really look like they're dancing. Personally, I prefer the style merchants.

I play Pachinko for a while. This is a great game. Shoot metal balls into the slots fast enough, win more metal balls and keep playing till you've lost 'em all. But, for once, I don't do this. I'm winning. I'm pressing random buttons, and the machine squeaks and squeals and there are little metal balls flying everywhere, then the machine is spewing them out at me. More and more and more, until the plastic bucket that I catch them in is overflowing and balls are spilling onto the floor and rolling off. I've never been in this situation before, so I ask another player what to do with the things. He smiles a lot, and has front teeth missing, and does not understand English at all. I use the universal language of miming and gesturing and talking too loud and I make myself understood. He points at a window.

Another toothless old guy shows me an array of crap plastic items. I mime that I don't want them but he insists I pick some, and points at another booth and says 'swap, swap.' I go over and the young woman in the other booth buys the crap off me. Nice deal. I end up with about fifty quid worth of yen. Dinner? Or some more drinks? Lol. I think we both know the answer again.

I pocket the yen and wonder what to do next. But I'm on a roll so there's really only one answer to this conundrum. More Pachinko! I go and get another 5k yen card. I push it into the machine and turn the handle on the machine that supplies the balls and they come flying out in a lovely arc, demonstrating the full beauty of projectile dynamics. The balls shush and shurr and there are little tunes and beeps and bells as they hit various objects, and balls come gushing out again. No matter what I do, it seems the thing spews out balls, to the extent that I wonder if it's broken, or been fixed by someone. My insomniac's dream world, like most people's, is a paranoid world.

I wander back to the *swap-swap* booth and, on my way, something bright catches my eye. A white flash somewhere behind the DDR machines. It's a woman's t-shirt, a particularly well-filled one, something I identify quickly even though it must enter my field of vision for less than a second. I prowl towards the back of the arcade where it came from. I catch a back view. It's like she's hiding from me. Turning a corner, I get a full frontal view and it's such a sight for sore eyes that it throws me for a moment. Then, as she dashes past, I realise it is *The Girl*. Is this some obsession I wasn't even aware of, a desire so deep I keep conjuring her up out of thin air?

This time I'm pretty sure I'm awake and not hallucinating, though. The maths hits me right away. Once or twice I could let pass by, but three times is a lady who's following me for some reason. Except I'm trailing her now and she's walking faster and faster as she feels me on her back. She breaks into a trot and then a run and I follow her all the way. She's fit, and the sight of her arms and legs pumping as she sprints away is pretty damn fine, but I concentrate on trying to keep up the pace. I'm no slacker, but she is fast, man.

And all the time as I'm pounding my feet into the concrete and feeling the strain on my knees, I'm thinking. The only sound is my heart pounding in my ears, and my breathing and the rushie-rush of the ball bearings in the cup I'm still holding, and occasionally, the sharp musical sound of a batch of the balls hitting the floor. I'm thinking that I don't believe in coincidences. I don't believe in much that lies outside of logic and physical reality. I'm thinking that this woman took my bag at the airport with a motive, and that whatever that was, that's why she's here now and why she doesn't want me to catch her up. I'm thinking that the more I analyse it, the more I think what I saw at

Marc's apartment was an hallucination; but what if I'm wrong? I'm out of breath and sick to the stomach. I'm thinking how I've slipped up, mentioning this trip to Uri. I'm happy to share the spoils with him; that's the deal between us on everything we do and I'm a man of my word. But I wish I'd acted first and seen him all right when I got back home. First mistake; the perfect crime is the one with no witnesses.

The Girl is pulling away from me and I'm on the verge of collapse. And I'm thinking that Uri surely doesn't know a woman like this. If he did he would have shown me photos, lied about how far he'd managed to get with her, told me stories. I'm thinking God knows what she wants from me but I don't think he's behind it. And I'm trying to kid myself she's after my body, and that this is the most convoluted chat up in history. That she is, quite literally, one those thrill of the chase people.

And then she's off round the corner and when I make it after her she's nowhere in sight. I stop, bending double with my hands on my knees, breathing hard. And I think, man, that bitch runs fast. And I think, man, I'd like to fuck her. And that's about all I think before I realise I better take a good ole puff on my inhaler before I drop down dead. And I do that, then I stagger to a bar on the corner, and order still holding that bucket of ball bearings (now half full) out in front of me, as if I think I can pay for my drinks with it.

I sleep that night – it must be the beer, that or the running. When I wake up, my mouth feels like moss has grown there overnight, and tastes much the same. I feel sick, and I want to go back to sleep but the idea I might have missed my slot with Reito wakes me right up. I've no fucking clue what the time is.

I get out of bed to check out the alarm clock. It's midday. I have no idea what time I got back or how long I slept for. I do not feel refreshed at all. In fact, I feel like someone drove a truck between my eyes. I think about the previous night. I remember drinking. I remember the arcades and my Pachinko wins and how *The Girl* turned up there. I can picture her sprinting ahead of me, arms and legs pumping like a trained athlete, her top riding up to show a tight, toned waist. *Rowr!* And I remember drinking again, once I'd lost her, in that sad, little bar. But that's all; I don't remember getting back to the hotel. It's like there's a dark patch of time missing from my life. I used to say people were full of shit when they said they forgot stuff when they drank. Shows how much I know.

I head out and into the afternoon. The sunlight isn't on my side today. It makes my eyes screw up tight and I can feel just how dry they are. There's still an hour to go before my appointment with Reito. I find a coffee house, a Starbucks FFS. These corporates are taking over the world. While I wait for time to pass before my meeting with Reito, I drink three large cappuccinos with extra shots and I can feel my heart pounding against my breastbone as if it's trying to escape.

I look around the room. It's fucked up to see the same furniture, those velvet chairs and chessboard tables, all this way away from their natural habitat. I still feel like I could drop to sleep on my feet, and yet I know if I tried to go back to bed, I'd end up studying the ceiling. Sleep is finished with me for now and this adds to the ethereal quality my life's taking on. Nothing feels solid. I don't know what it does feel like. Not a dream, not even that close to reality. It's like shadows, like whispers of life. I feel like I must have taken an hallucinogen and not realised. This has to be the worse hangover I've ever had.

I go through what I need to do. I read over the script I've written myself for the meeting. I sweat some more and the skin where my wrists meet my shirt comes up in red welts that I try, and fail, not to scratch. I know what I need to say, who I need to be, but I'm doubting my acting skills. I'm worried about forgetting my lines, changing the name of the company, giving myself away. I'm worried about what I may find when I see *The Dragon*. What security there will be. My hunch is that this guy doesn't have a clue what he's got, and won't have it properly protected. But you just never know.

I think about the missing hours from last night and wonder where they've gone, if there's some way of pulling them out from the depths of my pickled brain. It sends a thrill right through me as I remember *The Girl* again. It is a mixed up feeling of fear and attraction and confusion.

I have to pee, and when I wash my hands, I dry them and feel compelled to do the job again. I realise I'm going into OCD mode, something that's just on the edge of my energy, can become part of me if I let it. I resist rinsing them a third time, or tapping on each side of the sink exactly seven times. I don't let myself look at the floor as I walk, for cracks to avoid stepping on. I almost close my eyes as I find the purple velour chair I was sitting in and throw myself down. I stay there for five minutes, sitting back and relaxing, trying to find my centre, my zen lol.

Then I get up and go to the counter and get a double espresso with a big glass of water, and rush back to the safety of my chair. I down the coffee, in one, like it's tequila, and I pull a tequila face too, making a woman a few tables down stare, then giggle. I tip her a wink and she giggles again. I can't make up my mind if I love or hate this kinda behaviour, but I know from previous trips it's just a feature of young Japanese girls. I remember *Sour Face* and say a little prayer that she's not on duty this afternoon. Yesterday she was morning shift, but who knows, and I have a feeling that my name in her book wouldn't necessarily guarantee safe passage.

I pick up the water and drink that right down too, savouring the cold as it runs through my chest, pooling just behind my rib cage. I wipe sweat from my forehead with a tissue. I shove my papers in the briefcase and stand up, repeating the names from my cover story just one more time. Then I pull on my coat and head out. It is time.

I can't help but avoid the cracks in the pavement.

So, I'm sitting opposite President Reito of Isuchoto Games Corp and I am sweating my tits off. That, combined with the oil from my treatments, is making the colour run from my shirt. I swear, I can see the dye dripping down my wrists, the skin below red, white and blue like a mottled flag.

The Okinawa Dragon sits behind Reito, trapped inside a frame just to the right and above his head. I sneak a glance. *The Dragon* is blood red and rising, uncoiling, screaming out fire from its mouth and nostrils. I'm dying to find out what it can do but I can't read the rules text from where I'm sitting. I try not to stare at the card, and this effort, together with the caffeine and the lack of sleep, is sending me dizzy.

Reito is reading my document, and frowning a little, and I'm still doing cartwheels inside that it wasn't *Sour Face* at reception.

I say, 'Bro Toys UK is very keen to move our relationship with you forward. We have so many ideas that we think will work for you here in Japan.'

The lines in his forehead etch deeper, looking like they were drawn on with a 2H pencil.

And I say, 'The box contains our latest board game. *Wizards and Warriors*. It has elements of the card game but is almost more complex. We can help you with sales literature and, of course, we can provide everything in your local language.' I'm coming out with all this spiel, but I am thinking about the fire alarm I saw on my way in, on the wall of the corridor right by this office. Exactly where I need it to be.

I'm going on and on and I get the feeling he's not that interested. But I don't need him to be. I just need him to agree to look at the game overnight. It's rubbish. He will never take it on. Which is just as well, because it doesn't exist, and Bro Toys don't make it in English, never mind in Japanese. It is something I created in my shed with plastic, card and a good deal of superglue. I lost skin in the process but consider this a worthy sacrifice.

'I need time to consider such an offer,' Reito tells me.

I say, 'Of course.' I pause. Rub my chin. 'I could come back tomorrow,' I say.

He shakes his head and my heart drops through the floor. 'I am out the office, tomorrow,' he says. 'The day later?'

I scratch at my wrist. I smile. 'Of course.' And I hand him a few more imaginative little documents and close my briefcase.

I stand up and we both bow, then bow again, and I think I see him hold his hand out, and I make a grab for it and, rather embarrassed, we shake hands too. We are still bowing to each other like parts of an automated toy.

I pull away, still nodding my head, and I back towards the door. 'The rest room?' I say, pulling down the handle. He comes to the door to see me out, and points down the corridor. The men's room is a hop, skip and several jumps from the office; not what I was hoping for. I hold onto Reito's door long enough to check out the catch; a standard Yale. At least that fits the plan.

Reito's door sighs shut and I case the corridor, taking pigeon steps towards the loos in case I am being watched, or recorded on CCTV. I can feel myself frowning. The ladies is the right end of the corridor, opposite the office but, of course, it is a room with drawbacks as a hiding place for a man. There's a cupboard too, the cleaner's probably, right beside it. I check for observers and for cameras angled on the door, but all's clear so I give the handle a try. It is locked. That is not good.

I head towards the lift trying not to feel too beaten down. There are a few other offices on this level, including the one belonging to Reito's PA, an older woman with a girlie laugh that belies her years. Her giggling and flirting when I arrived for my appointment set my teeth on edge. I'm glad, at least, the offices are the kind with doors, not open plan or, almost worse, glass fronted. And in the twenty-seven steps it takes me to get to the lift, I feel a plan forming. One with flaws, I'll admit. But a plan is a plan is a plan. Innit?

Three in the afternoon, two days later, President Reito's office, Osaka, Japan, and I am bored of keeping you updated with my space-time now. Forty-eight hours have passed in a trance. I spent both nights with the American lads, in bars singing Karaoke, and smoking weed in their apartment. I've been shopping for gadgets and toys. I even shoplifted once. I've no need to with the budget Henri gave me, but it's

more fun sometimes. I've explored the castle and been for a trek in the hills. I've done pretty well everything there is to do here except sleep. The amount of sleep I've had is a big fat zero. Nada. nunca, rien, nacht, nothing. I feel like I've had an eyebath with crunchy peanut butter. I feel like I'm awake, except I also feel like I'm dreaming, and the fact I'm in Japan keeps making me laugh. The idea that I'm gonna steal *The Dragon* makes me giggle like a bastard. I'm so out of it, sitting here opposite Reito, there's a danger I might just lunge for the frame on the wall, stick my tongue out at the President, and run from the room. I hold back on this impulse.

Reito is looking at the board game I left for him and touching his chin. 'In-ter-resting,' he says, 'but not for us.'

I spout some crap about the things he is missing about *Wizards and Warriors*, and how our designers are happy to accept more input if it helps. I'm subdued, trying not to pile on the words per minute. I am looking at *The Dragon*, where it sits in the frame on his wall. I am looking for trip wires, for alarm lasers, clues about its security. I see nothing.

'I really do not think this game is for us,' he says. He is standing up.

I talk about future opportunities, our understanding of the gaming world, possibilities for games made to his spec. All the time I am counting yards from the front of his desk to the framed card, how many seconds it would take to get to it, one elephant, two elephants and all that crap.

Reito catches me, follows my gaze to the prize on his wall.

I sweat.

'Ah, the *Dragon*,' he says. 'Is a very powerful weapon. You know the game?'

I laugh so loud inside my head it's a surprise he can't hear it

'No,' I say.

Reito fills me in, bless him, but it's clear he doesn't know his arse from any of the hinge joints on his body as far as my world's concerned. 'A gift,' he says. 'I've been offered more than a thousand dollars for that card.'

I snort. I can't help myself. This is my *Sunflowers*, my *Venus de Milo*. I recover myself by saying what he is expecting. 'A thousand dollars? For a piece of card?'

'You would be surprised. But it's beside the point because I would never sell. To me, is priceless,' he says.

I nod. I could not agree more.

'Well, thank you for your time, Mr Robinson,' he says. He holds his hand out, western stylie. I bow, then take his hand, using the time to check the way the frame is attached to the wall. Simply, just a nail and a hook.

Then I am on my way out, making eye contact with him, bowing again and holding onto his office door. He is moving back towards his desk. I click on the latch with my card player deftness. Even I only just hear it catch.

'Thank you for your time,' I say. And he nods. I turn and check the exact position of the fire alarm again. I want to do this thing in one movement, one smooth sway from beginning to end like some old bloke doing Tai Chi.

Reito's door closes. I give him a moment, then I *(IN CASE OF FIRE) REMOVE HAMMER AND BREAK GLASS,* something I have always wanted to do. The alarm starts to squeal. Sprinklers erupt from the ceiling. I hadn't thought of that. I'm hoping there aren't any in the office, because *The Dragon cannot* get wet. I head across the corridor, following my plan. Except, in my half-real state, I get the trajectory wrong, and I am pulling at the cupboard door. It is still locked. I curse. I can hear movement in the offices around me. I duck into the ladies, praying it's empty.

I don't believe in God and he doesn't answer my prayers. Fair enough. There's someone in one of the stalls, and I can hear her scrabbling and panicking to respond to the alarm. I'm betting on the unquestioning obedience of the Japanese — it's something rooted in my plan. But maybe if she could just delay a little here, that would be very helpful of her. I dive into a cubical and close the door, just as I hear the chain flush and her door open. I lower the toilet seat and climb on top and hope she's not paying too much attention. I don't bother to pray this time.

I hear the main door go, and leave it a minute, counting elephants to slow myself down. Then I breathe and head out to the sink. I take a moment to clean the shirt dye from my wrist and the tops of my palm. Fucking cheap crap — I shoulda used the budget better. It's still making me itch, specially round the collar. I scrub my hands until I'm satisfied they are oil free. The skin is puckered and peeling in places by the time I'm done, but it's worth it. I'd kill myself if I got my greasiness all over *The Dragon*.

I look in the mirror and take some deep breaths. I am about to steal *The Okinawa Dragon*. In, out, with my breath. Deep yogic inhalations. Lateral thoracic breathing. And now.

My hand's on the door, but something's wrong. It's swinging towards me much faster than I'm pulling. Either (worse case) this is a security guard checking the toilets are empty or (best) a desperate woman running in and out before leaving. I swing with the door and stay behind it, watching with relief as a heavily pregnant lady runs to the nearest stall. She is quick, in and out, then back through the door without washing her hands, not noticing it is held open for her, nor the half inch of sole she could see if she looked down to the small gap above the floor.

I breathe again. I count. One elephant, two elephants... I make it a minute and think it's probably safe and time to make my move.

I peek out from behind the door and see Reito leaving. He shuts his door but doesn't stop to check it has locked. He walks with some urgency in his step and a hand above his hair to protect it from the water, which is spraying everywhere. He does not take *The Dragon*, which confirms to me it is wasted on him, and makes me feel better about what I'm planning to do. He'd just let it burn, in a fire? Miss Nakamura, his secretary, is following close behind. She doesn't do her duty and double check on her boss. They are both walking like people who know it's not a drill. I watch Reito's back disappear behind the fire door at the end of the corridor, then Nakamura's. The corridor is empty. Well, almost empty.

I smile to myself

I'm in Reito's office so quick I can still smell

his expensive cologne. I'm in there and I'm standing in front of *The Dragon* and it is magnificent. I read the details, learn for the first time what the card can actually do, and it is crushingly powerful, the way you'd expect. The card is so rare this information is unavailable. You can't even get a picture online.

To my relief, they skimped on getting a full sprinkler system and just did the corridor. *The Dragon* will not drown today. I reach for the frame, still slightly fearful of a laser activated alarm, of a cage falling on my head or the doors automatically locking like would happen if I tried to steal one of the artefacts in the Louvre. But I reach out and nothing happens. The sprinklers are in full fury outside the room, but in the office is all dry and peaceful.

And then I have it in my hand: *The Okinawa Dragon*. A one-off. There are so few things in the world that are truly unique and I can feel its heat in my palm. It's like the thing has a pulse.

So, I'm standing there, holding this card. It's the same as a million and one cards I've held before and yet it's not because it's *The Dragon*. A voice inside tells me to get the hell out of there, but I can't move. All I can do is look at the card.

I think about what I could do with it. Sell it to Henri? He'd give me a six figure sum, I don't doubt it. I could probably get more, auction it off in a hidden area of the interweb. All Henri's paid for is the trip and he has no hold over me or *The Dragon* and I've been straight up about this from the get go. But I can't help thinking: *If I did this deal, what would be left?* Then I think, *get the fuck out of here!*

I still don't move, though, and look closely at the art work. It's classy; the scales shimmer as you move it, the reds and oranges burn and bluster. I take in the text again, telling me how you can use the card. It's awesome. It would be hard to lose a game with this in your deck. I could keep it for myself. Not mention it to anyone and, one day, playing with mates I trust, I could pull it out, slam it down on the table with a flourish. *I summon The Okinawa Dragon!* That'd be something. Their faces!

The option I choose is, I put the card back. Then I put the frame back on the wall. Then I leave the room and head towards the fire exit.

Outside there are people everywhere. The entire tower block has emptied and is blocking the street. I know President Reito is there somewhere. Lost in the sea of his own employees he is reduced to the same as them. I make my way through the thick crowd then across the road.

I'm lying on my hotel bed thinking about *The Dragon*. It sends a thrill up inside me every time I remember how it felt in the palm of my hand.

I need something to take the edge off this feeling — alcohol would do. I call Marc from the phone in my room and we arrange to meet in the *Very Funny* Karaoke place in an hour's time. I can't wait that long so I grab a bottled beer from the minibar and get into the shower drinking.

I almost surprise myself by remembering the way to the Karaoke bar without too much trouble. I get there ahead of Marc and the other boys and am seated by a *Very Funny* girl. She brings me a rum and coke and places it carefully on a doily and I smile as a businessman crucifies 'He ain't heavy, he's my brother.' And it's while I'm grinning that I spot her; the actress/model/suitcase thief from the airport, sitting a couple of tables away, being waited on by her very own *Very Funny* girl. This makes my breathing faster because she looks so sexy; wearing jeans and a tight pink tee. But also because I know it's all wrong, wrong, wrong.

She turns and sees me, picks up her drink and moves to my table. 'Well hello again,' she says, narrowing her eyes. 'You're the guy from the airport, right?'

And the rest, I think, but I just nod.

'What a coincidence.'

And I think, yeah, maybe that's all it is. Although I know that's just my penis talking, trying to persuade me. 'Hey Jack, look, seriously man this is fine, honestly, it is all right and what you should focus on is trying to *do* this girl.' He can be a real dick sometimes.

I'm sipping my drink, trying to come up with the right opener for this situation. Whatever this woman wants with me, I don't want to embarrass myself with a come here often or a nice girl like you place like this cliché. In the end I settle for 'Hi. Jack,' and hold my hand out to her. If she notices the pun, she is polite enough to ignore it.

'Donna,' she says, shaking my hand. She has a firm handshake.

'That's a good old English name. I'm not sure it suits you.'

She smiles. 'Well, you don't really know me, do you?'

'You have a point. I don't know anything about you. For all I know it could be a fake name.'

That makes her laugh, and both of our girls tell us it's 'very funny ' and giggle with hands held over mouths.

I take a long drink and she lights a cigarette and I say, 'Why did you run away from me the other day?'

She takes a drag and screws up her face, looking puzzled and amused (and very hot) all at the same time. 'At the airport?'

If she's faking then she's a *very* good actress.

'At the arcade,' I say.

She laughs and it's a good sound; a noise I could get used to hearing. 'I don't do arcades. You must be mistaken.'

I want to believe her, this sexy bitch who keeps turning up wherever I go. The scene in front of me, the Japanese clichés of business-men, singing Karaoke badly, the young, cute *Very Funny* girls, and this unfeasibly attractive woman looking right into my eyes, it's like something out of a fantasy and I do wonder if this is all some invention of my inner psyche, a trip, or a flashback from something I've taken on one of the many crazy nights of my life. The whole scene is making my head spin.

* * *

An hour or so later and I'm drunk enough that I begin to chat up this Donna girl, forget about my suspicions of her motives. I begin to think only about the possibility of sex.

Of course, I have rivals. The boys arrived and you should have seen the way their eyes widened when they took in Donna. It was almost funny to watch them assessing the situation, trying to work out if we were together, or just flirting. It wasn't long, though, before they relaxed, stopped giving a shit, and were trying to get in there anyway. Marc was the first to have to a go. When he realised he was getting nowhere, Chuck took up the baton, then Ted.

But Donna isn't taking much notice of the yanks. She is all about me. She acts like she doesn't hear when one of that lot makes a joke and yet she laughs loudly at me. A voice in my head tells me this is not so different from the *Very Funny* girls. A voice in my penis insists it is. Guess which one I'm listening to at this stage. Lol. I think we both know the answer. And the thing is, she's funny. Very funny. And she makes me laugh. I know my own limitations and resisting the charms of a girl this attractive, who makes me laugh, well, that's way beyond them.

She wants to duet with me; *Something Stupid*, that Sinatra one with Nancy when you sing a weird off-harmony. It's the most dangerous

Karaoke song in the world. You really gotta be able to sing to carry this off. You'd be mad to take it on, if you got any pride whatsoever. Mad, or drunk. Or horny. I am a mixture of all those things when she suggests it, and up I get, and over we both go.

She can sing. I can sing and, even though I'm drunk, I look around the room and I can tell we're doing okay by people's reactions. Then I forget about them. I just look at her. She looks at me. 'And then I go and spoil it all by saying something stupid like I love you…' she sings and I am flying with the attention I'm getting from her, losing the plot. Mr Penis is so bloody happy he could burst and quite possibly will if we don't get it on tonight.

Of course, when we finish, our *Very Funny* girls go mad. And I wonder how insane they would go if we were to kiss. If we were to get it on. What if we left to together? I think if I shagged her, their heads might explode. Donna touches my hand.

Mr Penis does a little dance

She smiles at me and it's all I can do not to

grab her and kiss her right there. But I check myself. This is too easy. She is just too darn hot. There really is something going on here, no matter how hard Mr Penis is trying to convince me otherwise. I think she's a little gobsmacked when I turn away from her and head back to my seat.

I ask my *Very Funny* girl to get a cocktail for everyone in the room. B52s all round. I stand on my chair and shout 'Milky Bars are on me!' Screams of assent from the Americans. The locals in the bar look confused, then go back to their conversations, but when the drinks start arriving they realise what's going on. I'm toasted from all over the bar and I feel like the King of Japan. Donna is heading back towards me and I'm wondering what she really wants, and how to make my next move and find out. I am determined not to invite her back to my room at the hotel.

I'm so wasted by the time I get back to my hotel that I don't remember the journey. Of course, Donna is with me.

'I am going to fix you a cock-tail,' she says, trying an American accent on for size, slurring and stressing the two syllables at the end of the sentence. She sways into the bathroom and comes back with the two plastic cups they leave for you to rinse your mouth with. She is holding them open ends together, a makeshift cocktail shaker. And I can hardly stop laughing to breathe for a while. Told you she made me laugh.

And then she's handing me this vile-coloured concoction and I'm drinking it. It tastes as bad as it looks but I know it's full of alcohol so I keep knocking it back.

And then I'm feeling very sleepy. Really fucking sleepy, so tired my eyes are going. And then…

I wake up with one banger of a headache. It feels like someone took out my brain and cleaned out the inside of my head with a wire brush, before pushing the grey matter back in through one of my ears. My eyesight is all over the place, blurred then focused, blurred then focused, and I know right away I'm not waking from a normal sleep. The bitch slipped me something in that ridiculous cocktail she mixed. Rohipnol or similar.

She's still here, standing over me, coming in and out of focus. I open my mouth to speak but my throat is dry and my voice creaks.

'So you date raped me, did ya?'

Even now she smiles. Smiles behind the gun she's holding. 'You could say that.'

I rub my eyes, hoping to erase the picture in front of me but having no such luck. I think about panicking but I don't have the energy. I think it's to do with the drugs she's given me. I know I should be scared but I'm not capable. 'I was ready, willing and able baby. Really, you coulda saved your drugs for recreational use, or your next victim.' I yawn. 'You were onto a dead cert.'

She laughs at that but it's a nervous laugh.

'Hey, I'm the one the wrong end of that gun.' And, again, I find I don't feel scared. I almost want to but only numbness comes.

'The card,' she says.

'What card?'

'You know what card.'

A smile pulls on my lips despite the situation. 'I didn't take it.'

She looks at me, that studying appraisal she's good at. And I can tell by the way her face is changing that she thinks I'm telling her the truth. Hell, she's probably been through the apartment and frisked me to death so she must have a clue it's not here.

'Search me if you like.' I hold up both hands. 'Baby.' I wink.

She doesn't take me up on my offer but rushes around the room throwing my stuff all over the place. 'It fucking has to be here somewhere.' The stress on her voice is palpable. She's running around the place totally manic and off her box. Then she stops dead. 'The safe,' she says. She is staring at it. 'Open the fucking safe.'

I shrug and rub at my eyes. I walk over and type in the code — the door springs open. She pushes me aside and, still shaking the gun in my vague direction, rifles through its contents. My wallet — pulling out all the money and throwing my credit cards on the floor until it's completely empty. My passport — opening it up at every page then turning it upside down and giving it a good shake. Something about the concentrated look on her face rouses a memory, a picture in my head. And I feel like I just woke up. And I realise why this woman looked so familiar.

Uri keeps a family portrait in the warehouse, on his desk, a cute little picture from years ago of him with his parents and little sister. In that photo she must be twelve at most. And, boy, she's grown up since. I knew it had been a mistake to tell Uri.

She turns to me. The look on her face tells a whole story. 'It's not here,' she says.

'I know.' And I'm laughing now. 'I didn't take it.'

She stands staring me out for a moment or two. I know now she's Uri's sister, just a good looking amateur, and I know she won't shoot. The gun's probably fake. She turns and storms out, slamming the door on her way like the teenager I remember.

I'm laughing so hard I think I might wet my pants. I'm falling back on the bed holding my tummy with how funny it is.

I told you she makes me laugh.

Before I go, I head back to Reito's office one more time. I have to. My stay here has the feel of a dream about it or, more than that, an acid trip; having a gun pointed at me, meeting a woman right out of my dirtiest fantasies and having her turn out to be a double agent and point a gun at me. All very James Bond.

Not to mention holding *The Dragon* in the palm of my hand. Feeling the beat of its heart. Man oh man.

It's like a lucid dream still coming at me through a haze of jetlag and prolonged lack of sleep, not to mention the slight rohipnol mist that still settles over my head. Who woulda thought a girl like that would date rape me? It makes me hard still, just thinking about it. I fantasise about what she might have done to me when I was out of it. It's more fun to make it up than imagine her rooting round the room.

I have to go back to the Isuchoto Games offices, I have to see the bricks and mortar, touch the cold concrete. I have to remind myself it all really happened. I remember the test to see if you are awake. The brain is good at creating the illusion of wet surfaces, like damp grass, but it's not so good at rough, dry things and it doesn't like faking pain or blood. Pinch yourself is not so far from the truth. I scrape my hand against the side of the building until it grazes and I feel the heat and the pain. I suck on the wound and savour the sweetness of my own blood. It tastes real enough.

I stand at the base of the huge tower block, staring up as it shoots into the sky, and there I go with it. I could steal *The Okinawa Dragon*. Sometimes, it is enough to know.